A Murder of Crows

Ben could feel the blood beating in his chest as he thought about what came next. The soldiers as still as death, but not yet dead. The crows perched on broken arms and legs. Black feathers slowly covered the men's bodies. Then he heard the screams of the soldiers as the crows pecked at their open wounds.

'It's not the kind of death you'd wish on anyone,' Mrs Carter said.

Look out for other exciting
stories in the *Shades* series:

A Murder of Crows

Penny Bates

Published by Evans Brothers Limited
2A Portman Mansions
Chiltern St
London W1U 6NR

First published in 2004

British Library Cataloguing in Publication Data
Bates, Penny
A murder of crows. - (Shades)
1. Young adult fiction
I. Title
823. 9'2 [J]

ISBN 0 237 52648 4

Series Editor: David Orme
Editor: Julia Moffatt
Designer: Rob Walster

Chapter One

The crows looked down from the top of the great oak tree. For once they were silent, like witches about to cast a dark spell. Their sharp eyes watched the ground where the injured crow was waiting. Waiting for their verdict.

The injured crow hopped clumsily from side to side, trying to fly. It croaked loudly

to the black shapes above. There was a
sudden beating of wings high in the
branches. It was the sign. The crows in the
oak were the Keepers of Crow Law. They
were judge and jury. It was up to them now.
They raised their necks and gave a loud
caw. They had reached their verdict.
At last.

The old man watching from his hiding
place knew this was a trial like any other.
A chance to be found not guilty. A time to
live, or a time to die. But now it was over.
The injured bird had broken Crow Law. It
would have to be punished for its crime.

There was a slow flapping of wings as
the dark shapes came down from the sky.
They swooped through the air, their
blackness cutting out all light. The old man
shivered as he stared through his binoculars.
There seemed to be hundreds of crows. He'd

seen the jet-black cloud of beaks and claws before. The strong claws and knife-like beaks were just right for tearing flesh.

Some people said there was no such thing as Crow Law.

'It's survival of the fittest,' the old man's daughter liked to say. 'A sick crow is a danger to the flock and so the others finish it off. You and your old wives' tales, Dad!'

Only the old man knew better. There were many trials on Crow Hill. Many small white skulls now lay beneath the trees. It was the way of crows. They always cast out bad blood.

The young bird didn't move as two crows landed in a rush of black wings. Another shiver ran down the old man's spine. He had seen this before and could not forget how cruel it was. Terror filled the victim's face as the other crows closed in. The guilty crow may have been caught smashing another crow's eggs or killing young in a nest. The other crows would break its wings if they witnessed the crime. Then Crow Law would decide the rest.

The two crows struck first. One crow stood on each side of the bird as they pecked out its eyes. The guilty bird's head jerked from side to side as the crows stabbed and pulled. Then one crow stopped and gave a grisly caw. The blinding was over. Then the rest of the crows dived down. They threw the bird from side to side. They plucked its feathers and tore strips off its flesh. The old man bit his lip. He prayed for the bird to die fast to end the pain.

'It's not survival of the fittest,' he said, as he watched its skull pecked bare. 'It's revenge!'

Chapter Two

The new Meadow Estate was a mile from
the old man's hide-out as the crow flies.

'These houses are no better than
shoeboxes!' the old man complained as
he marched up the path to number 21.
'They're all piled on top of each other
with walls as thin as cardboard. Why
did they dig up all those trees and

fields to build a place like this?'

'Is that you, Dad?' called a voice from
the back garden. 'Come and see what
I've planted.'

William Turner's angry face creased into
a smile when he saw the primroses. Their
yellow petals looked like flecks of sunlight
against the dark earth. The woman smiled
too as she admired her work.

'I thought you'd like them, Dad,'
she said. 'A little reminder of
Yew Tree Cottage.'

William took a deep breath to stop a
tear falling.

'Those primroses are little beauties,
Rose,' he said quietly. 'There'll be primroses
and daffodils out now at Yew Tree Cottage.
The garden will be at its best. I do miss it!'

'I know, Dad,' Rose replied gently. 'But
it's time to make a fresh start. You said

yourself that the cottage seemed a different place when Mum died. I know you loved the garden but it was just too big for one person to keep tidy. I'm pleased you came to live with Luke and me. We can help each other.'

William sighed and held Rose's hand.

'We've had more than our fair share of troubles,' he said, shaking his head. 'I just hope that Luke will get over it. Losing his Grandma was bad enough, but then to lose his dad...'

Rose stared hard at the primroses with tears in her eyes.

'That's why I need you here,' Rose replied. 'Luke's a real handful at school now. The teachers say he lashes out at everyone. We have to stop his anger getting the better of him.'

William nodded, and gave a long sigh.

'Can't have the boy getting into any more bother,' he said firmly. 'I'll keep an eye on him.'

A black shadow swooped across the flowers as a crow landed on the fence. It tilted its head to one side as it watched a worm slide over the soil below. The old man looked up and saw the blood on its beak.

'By the way, there's a family from Birmingham moving into the house next door,' Rose said brightly. 'A mother and son. I hope the boy's Luke's age. It'd be nice if they could be friends.'

Chapter Three

Ben Carter first saw the crow when he and
his mother were putting up curtains in his
new bedroom. It was sitting on the roof of
the garden shed and flapping its wings,
as if asking to be fed. The crow was
watching the house. It had sharp eyes
and it cawed loudly.

Ben couldn't take his eyes off the crow.

He'd never thought anything could be so ugly and yet so beautiful at the same time. The bird's dark shape made him think of terrible things like death and the devil's magic. But each black feather had a deep blue gloss that shone like sapphires.

'Stop dreaming, Ben, and pass me another curtain hook!' Mrs Carter snapped, as she struggled with the curtains.

'But there's a crow in the garden, Mum!' Ben replied. 'He keeps looking at me and calling as if there's something he wants to say.'

Mrs Carter looked outside.

'The countryside's lovely,' she said. 'Not a tower block in sight. Nothing but hills and fields as far as the eye can see. It's a shame that horrible crow has to spoil the view. It reminds me of the starlings we left behind in Birmingham.'

Ben frowned as he thought about the comfortable house in Birmingham. It was only a bus ride away from the city centre. Living in the country wouldn't be the same. It was too quiet, and the new house was miles from anywhere. His parents' divorce had changed everything and it wasn't fair!

'We'll be moving somewhere smaller,' Mrs Carter told Ben after his dad left. 'It'll be good for both of us to move to the countryside. We need a fresh start.'

Ben just wanted his mother and father to make their peace. He kept telling himself that they could all be a happy family again. But then his father moved in with a woman who lived in the next street. There could be no happy ending. There was a tired look on his mother's face when she talked about a fresh start. Ben knew she was hurting and had to move away.

'Why can't I have a new uniform?' Ben sighed when his mother said she couldn't afford to buy a blazer for the new school. 'I know my old clothes still fit but they won't help me to fit in! I'm fourteen and I need *some* street cred!'

The thought of trying to make new friends scared him. It had been hard to get to know people at his old school. He was the smallest boy in his year and that was a problem. It wasn't cool to be small and he didn't seem to be growing. Some of the boys made jokes. Ben couldn't stand it.

'Who'll want to speak to me?' he shouted down the phone at his father. 'A short kid with a funny accent and no dad!'

At least the crow looked friendly. It flew onto the bedroom window-sill and started tapping against the pane. Ben tapped back.

'Don't encourage it!' Mrs Carter said. 'Crows are bad luck.'

The bird eyed her coldly. It tilted its head to one side, as if it was thinking.

'He's got bristles at the bottom of his beak!' Ben laughed. 'Just like a moustache! He's cute.'

'I don't like the way it's looking at me!' Mrs Carter complained. 'As if it's hungry. I may be forty but I'm not dead meat!'

The crow replied by pecking at the window with its beak. It looked like it was trying to break the glass.

'Mum, he *must* be hungry if he fancies biting you!' Ben replied. 'But what do you mean by dead meat?'

'Well if you'd read the bird book I bought you last Christmas you would know that your friend here is a carrion crow!' Mrs Carter said. 'That means he eats dead flesh and he's not fussy where it comes from.'

Ben pulled a face as he imagined the crow's last meal. It was probably a dead rabbit full of maggots.

'At least crows keep the roads clean,' Ben said, as he tried to see the crow in a better light. 'There are lots of animals killed by cars every day. With crows around, they soon disappear!'

The bird croaked. Then it tapped at Mrs Carter's reflection on the glass as if it would tear her apart.

'You've got a point,' Mrs Carter agreed, 'but that's why there were always crows around battlefields. They pecked at the soldiers' corpses. Crows are clever birds but they're not always clever enough to tell the difference between the dying and the dead.'

Ben looked at the crow and thought of

his own flesh being split open by the sharp beak. He saw the fear on the soldiers' faces as the black shadows dived to the ground. The men were too sick to defend themselves. They were shivering as they lay in the mud and too weak to move.

Ben could feel the blood beating in his chest as he thought about what came next. The soldiers as still as death, but not yet dead. The crows perched on broken arms and legs. Black feathers slowly covered the men's bodies. Then he heard the screams of the soldiers as the crows pecked at their open wounds.

'It's not the kind of death you'd wish on anyone,' Mrs Carter said.

Chapter Four

The crow appeared at Mrs Carter's kitchen window the next day. Ben's breakfast was waiting on the table. It was his favourite meal of sausage, bacon and eggs.

'Hurry up, Ben, or your food will get cold!' Mrs Carter called. The crow called too. It gave a loud kraa – kraa – kraa as it stared at the meat on Ben's plate.

'Hello Joe crow!' Ben joked as he sat down to eat. 'I bet you'd like a piece of bacon.'

Ben held up a piece of meat for the bird to see. The crow stood still as stone, watching him.

'Don't start feeding that bird!' Mrs Carter shouted as she set off for the shops. 'And make sure you wash up!'

'OK, Mum,' Ben muttered as he started to cut a sausage into small pieces. 'Don't worry. This plate will be wiped clean when you get back!'

Ben opened the window gently and placed a slice of sausage on the sill. The crow watched him nervously. Then it took a step back, as if frightened.

'Come on Joe!' Ben whispered. 'Don't play hard to get. Look at this meat. It's still warm. Just how you like it!'

The bird hopped forward. Its eyes were fixed on the sausage.

'That's it, Joe,' Ben said quietly. 'Don't be scared.'

Then the crow snatched the meat. It watched Ben's face as it ate. Ben smiled. He was pleased the crow trusted him. It swallowed the piece of sausage. Then the black beak asked for more.

'Here you are, Joe. Let's see if you like bacon fat,' Ben said when the last of the sausage had gone. 'Take it from my hand.'

The bird stared at Ben's hand with a beady eye. Its head was tilted to one side as it waited. Ben wiggled the fat between his fingers to make the crow think it was a worm. The black beak bobbed up and down and Ben wondered if his fingers were about to become food. Then the beak stabbed quickly and the fat slid down the bird's throat. Ben smiled again. He was happy to have found a friend.

'How cute!' said a cold, hard voice as the crow suddenly flapped away. 'But that's not a pet, city kid. It's a crow!'

Ben saw the tall boy out of the corner of his eye. He was standing in the kitchen doorway with a knowing grin on his face. Ben felt small and stupid.

'I'm Luke,' the tall boy laughed as Ben went red. 'Grandad told me to come round. You're starting at my school on Monday, Crow Boy! But don't worry. Your secret's safe with me!'

Chapter Five

'Do I have to catch the school bus with Luke?' Ben asked.

'Of course you do!' Mrs Carter said as she brushed a black feather from Ben's shirt. 'It was kind of him to offer to go with you on your first day. You might be friends. You're lucky to be living next door to a boy your own age.'

Ben frowned. He didn't feel lucky at all.

'Luke's older than me,' Ben replied as he tried to find a reason not to be friends. 'Almost fifteen!'

'Well, he's here now, and it's time to go,' Mrs Carter added as she straightened his tie. 'I must get off to the job centre. It's the early bird that catches the worm!'

Ben could see his bird sitting on the garden fence. The sausage and bacon had gone down well again. The crow had taken food from Ben's hand.

'Morning, Mrs Carter!' came Luke's cheerful voice from the hallway. 'How are you settling in?'

Ben sighed as his mother welcomed Luke with a smile. She liked Luke and said he was such a polite young man.

'Is Ben ready yet?' Luke asked. 'Don't worry, Mrs Carter. I'll look after him!'

It was a long walk to the school bus-stop on the edge of the estate. Luke marched ahead with his sports bag thrown over one shoulder.

'What's up, Crow Boy?' he asked as Ben struggled to keep up. 'You city kids just aren't fit! The country air will do you good. Take a deep breath and you might just grow!'

'But *you're* not a country boy either!' Ben replied. 'You live on a brand new housing estate.'

Luke stopped sharp and dropped his bag to the ground. There was a flash of temper in Luke's eyes and Ben stopped too, suddenly afraid.

'I used to be a country boy!' Luke snapped. 'I lived on a farm until Dad died.'

There was a tear in Luke's eye. Ben stared at the ground. He wanted to break the silence, but didn't know what to say.

'My dad doesn't live with us anymore,'
Ben said finally. 'He just left one day.
What happened to your dad?'

Luke kicked his sports bag as the anger
came back.

'Died of a broken heart,' Luke muttered.
'Dad had to help kill his own sheep and
cattle when the foot and mouth came to
our farm. He had to watch them burn on
huge bonfires. The smoke hung over the
fields for days. There was no clean air
to breathe. Only the smell of burning
skin and bones. Then we had no animals
to sell and no cows to milk. The bills
couldn't be paid and we sold the farm.
Dad said he didn't want to live if he
couldn't farm. He killed himself, so
he could die a farmer. My dad was a
countryman. A proud man.'

'I'm sorry,' Ben said softly. 'I hadn't realised—'

'What would a city kid know!' Luke said sharply. 'City people think the countryside is just about flowers and little white lambs in spring! I bet you think it's going to be one long picnic living here. All fluffy white clouds and no worries!'

Ben felt stupid again. He remembered finding out about the countryside from picture books when he was small. In the stories there were little red hens in the country, and fresh eggs for tea. The skies were always blue and there was always a happy ending. Ben looked up at the sky as Luke slung his bag over his shoulder. There wasn't any blue to be seen. Only grey.

'Time to grow up, city kid!' Luke said as he swung his bag onto his shoulder. 'Get walking or we'll be late.'

'Here's the new boy!' Luke shouted when they joined the school bus queue.

A group of teenagers wearing baggy shirts and torn school ties stared hard at Ben. Some of the boys grunted and Ben nodded back.

'But wait till you hear this!' Luke said, bursting into laughter. 'He's a city kid with a pet crow! I've even heard him talking to it. How stupid can you get?'

Ben's face burned red as the other boys started to laugh. He lowered his head as the girls at the bus stop started to giggle. The grey sky was closing in now. The happy ending moving out of reach.

'Sad!' the girls agreed. 'Bet that crow's the only bird he can get!'

'That's right!' Luke added. 'With a face like that the new boy's got nothing to crow about. I suppose he has to take what he can get!'

Ben put up with the jokes and laughter until the bus arrived. His head was buzzing with all the words he wished he had said. He would have tried to fight back at his old school. He would not have let them win. But here it was different. He was a city kid who could not understand their rules. So he said nothing and hung his head in shame.

Then the bus doors opened and he dared to look up. There was a clatter of feet as everyone rushed forward to get the best seats. It was then that Ben saw her. She stood apart from the rest of the girls. The pretty red-haired girl smiled shyly at Ben and he smiled back. For a moment Ben thought she was about to speak. He took a step towards her, but stopped when he saw Luke watching.

'You can look but don't touch!' Luke hissed as he pushed Ben towards the bus. 'That's Ruth, and I fancied her first.'

Chapter Six

'I think it's cute of him to want to look after a crow!' Ruth said as Luke and his friends made jokes about Ben. 'It shows a caring side.'

Luke sneered, but stopped as he caught sight of Ruth's green eyes. She smiled as she bit into a roll. She was so beautiful and wouldn't hurt a fly.

'Move over, Luke! Crow Boy's coming over with his plate of chips,' another boy hissed as Ben looked for somewhere to sit. 'Over here, Ben!' the boy yelled. 'I'm Gary. Make yourself at home.'

Ruth wanted to know about the crow. She asked if it had a name and how old it was.

'He's called Joe,' Ben answered. 'But I don't know how old he is. He was in our garden when we moved in.'

Ruth's eyes gleamed as Ben spoke. Her cheeks went pink every time Ben looked at her.

'I know how old that bird is,' Luke shouted. 'When Mum and I moved into the new house the builders were still working on the estate. The place was a mess. There was mud everywhere and flocks of crows. The builders used to feed them in their tea breaks. Then the site manager found a young crow. It was alone and hungry. The builders fed it on worms.'

'So that was Joe!' Ben said. 'We moved in when all the houses were finished, so Joe must be almost a year old.'

Luke frowned. He didn't like the way Ruth smiled every time Ben spoke. He didn't like the way Ben leaned towards her. Luke's fingers closed into a fist beneath the table. He wanted to punch Ben away.

'Poor little Joe was an orphan,' Ruth said, sweeping her red hair away from her face. 'At least there's a happy ending now he's with Ben!'

'I don't think you know much about crows, Ruth,' Gary added as he stuffed his mouth with chips. 'I would have smashed that fledgling on the head. The only good crow is a dead one!'

Luke watched Ben and Ruth angrily. They both looked shocked at the thought of killing a baby crow. He didn't like the way Ruth touched her hair when she spoke to Ben. Or her sudden interest in a stupid city kid with a pet crow. It was time to get Ruth back on his side where she belonged.

'Gary's right. Crows are vermin!' Luke said. 'They damage crops, steal eggs and attack sheep and lambs. One morning my dad found one of his sheep half-dead. She had fallen and hurt her leg. The crows had found her in the night and pecked her eyes out!'

Luke shook his head sadly as he waited for a reaction on Ruth's face. Her skin turned white against her red hair. She swallowed hard, as if she felt sick. Luke grinned to himself. Now Ruth would be his again! She had to be. He smacked his lips at the thought of going out with her. He only had to ask.

'Crows have to be kept down,' Luke continued. 'That's why farmers shoot them. It's quick and clean and the crows don't suffer.'

'Perhaps you'd better think hard about your crow, Ben,' Gary added as he stole one of Ben's chips. 'I bet it's tearing the skin off a weak lamb right now. You can borrow my air pistol anytime!'

Chapter Seven

Ben didn't want to talk to his mother about school. He couldn't tell her that he wasn't Ben anymore but Crow Boy. He was the soft city kid who didn't fit in. At least he could talk to Joe.

The crow was always waiting for Ben when he came home from school. It was good to find him there.

'You're a good friend, Joe,' Ben liked to say when the crow flew to him and landed on his shoulder. 'A good listener.'

The bird followed Ben everywhere.

'Joe copies everything I do!' Ben explained when Mrs Carter spotted the crow following her son into the kitchen. 'If I eat, he eats. When I do my homework he taps my pen with his beak! Joe's really special. He's not like other crows.'

Ben's mother was worried. She wanted Ben to spend time with Luke and not with a filthy crow.

'He's a clever bird!' William Turner called over the fence as Ben weeded the garden, watched closely by Joe. 'Looks like he wants to help!'

'I think so too!' Ben replied. 'We're both in trouble with Mum. Doing the garden is one way of cheering her up!'

Ben bent down to pull up another weed. The crow copied him by plucking at some grass.

'Crows are clever,' the old man continued. 'That's why they're not fooled by scarecrows. I've often seen crows sitting on a scarecrow's head!'

Ben nodded as he watched Joe tug at some dandelion leaves.

'If Joe wants me when I'm in the house, he taps on the window,' Ben said proudly. 'And when he finds a tough seed to crack he holds it with one foot and breaks it open with his beak. He's always working things out for himself!'

William was happy to talk to someone who liked animals and birds.

'I watched some crows by the seashore once,' William added. 'They were picking up small crabs. The crows flew high in the air, then dropped the crabs on hard ground to break their shells open! Crows are clever birds. I just wish Luke would take more of an interest in birds of the feathered kind!'

Ben took a deep breath at Luke's name. The old man was kind and friendly. If only Luke could be the same!

'Don't let Luke get the better of you,' William said quietly, as if reading Ben's mind. 'He likes to throw his weight around a bit.'

'Luke told me about the builders feeding the crows,' Ben said, changing the subject. 'It must have been noisy with so many crows around.'

'It made the front page of the local paper!' William laughed. 'The reporter used the headline A MURDER OF CROWS! I ask you! Of course some people wanted to leave as soon as they'd moved in. They said it was like a scene from a horror film. After the builders had gone the crows kept tapping on the windows asking for food. Some of the children were terrified and their mothers wanted the birds shot.'

'I suppose there wasn't much point washing cars on a Sunday with so many crows around!' Ben joked.

Joe flew up and settled on Ben's shoulder.

'The pest control men sorted things out in the end,' William said. 'They put up nets in front of the windows to stop the crows tapping. Finally the crows realised there was no more food and flew away.'

Ben wondered why Joe had stayed on the estate.

'Your bird was young,' William answered. 'He was a bit of an outsider too, because he liked being fed by hand. I gave him the odd titbit when the builders left. But it's a shame he never found a mate. Some people say it's bad luck to see a single crow. Perhaps we'd better watch out!' They laughed. The crow moved its head. Just like a nod.

Chapter Eight

'Grandad said he had a chat with you about crows!' Luke said loudly. He wanted other boys in the school yard to hear. 'He thinks you're *such* a nice boy!'

Ben took a step back but wanted to run away.

'I suppose he told you some tall tales about Crow Law. He told me all that stupid stuff when I was a little kid. I bet you believed him!'

Gary came over, smirking. He stopped and spat on the ground.

'It's about time we made some feathers fly, Luke,' he muttered. 'Crow Boy has asked Ruth to come and see his little black pet this weekend. Ruth thought it was a *lovely* idea. I think Crow Boy fancies her! I bet he's going to ask her out.'

Luke moved slowly towards Ben, his face full of hate.

Ben waited for a fist to find his face, but nothing happened. Luke had other plans. This time he wanted to get his claws into someone and skin them alive. He wanted to cause real pain. A fist in the face would be over too quickly.

'I told you to stay away from Ruth!' Luke growled into Ben's ear. 'I said I had plans for her, but you thought you could get in there first!'

Then Luke folded his arms and nodded for Gary to begin.

'I don't fancy Ruth!' Ben spluttered as Gary held an arm around his neck. 'And I've never even heard of Crow Law.'

Luke grinned as Gary tightened his grip.

'We ought to string you up like farmers hang up dead crows!' Gary hissed in Ben's ear. 'String you up until you rot!'

Ben started to gag as Gary gripped his throat. The yard was spinning and Ben felt his knees start to buckle beneath him. He wanted to scream but could hardly breathe.

'We could hang you on Crow Hill!' Luke roared in Ben's ear. 'That's where Grandad says the crows hold their courts of law!'

'Unless you confess your crimes and agree to shoot your pet crow,' Gary said.

He let go of Ben's throat. 'Then we might just leave you alone.'

'Possibly...' Luke jeered as he pressed his fingers into Ben's face. 'I'd like to see that crow's head on a stick! Drop him now, Gary, and we'll see what he has to say...'

Chapter Nine

Mrs Carter looked at the bruises on Ben's neck when he came down to breakfast the next morning.

'They look sore,' she said gently. 'I'll go to see the headteacher if you get hurt again playing football. I know teachers can't have eyes everywhere but that kind of tackling really shouldn't be allowed!

If that's what really happened...'

Ben said nothing as he opened the window to pass Joe some toast. He watched Joe peck at the food and then preen his feathers before asking for more. Joe wasn't greedy now. He didn't need to snatch and steal. Ben knew the bird trusted him.

'Luke and Gary are coming round this morning,' Ben said quickly, as if it meant nothing. 'We'll play a few computer games if that's all right with you.'

'I don't mind. I've got to do the weekend shopping,' Mrs Carter replied. 'You can have the house to yourself. I'm really pleased you've made some new friends.'

Ben's heart sank as his mother drove away. He'd hoped she'd be staying at home to work in the garden. Then Joe would be safe. Ben dug his fingers into the palms of his hands when he thought about what he'd agreed to do. How could he be so weak? What kind of person offered to shoot their pet crow to save their own skin? But he knew there was no other way to get Luke off his back.

Joe was sitting on the birdbath in the garden when Luke and Gary arrived. Gary was carrying an air pistol, his mouth fixed in a sneer. Joe stopped splashing in the water and watched him. Ben prayed that his crow might be as clever as the birds William had mentioned. If only Joe knew the difference between a rake and a gun like the crows that lived on farms!

'Let's see how well you can shoot, Crow Boy!' Gary said as he gave Ben the pistol.

'Aren't these illegal?' Ben asked, trying to find a way out.

'Why? Is Crow Boy frightened?' sneered Gary. 'I'd get him on the birdbath if I were you. It's easy shooting sitting ducks!'

Ben started to shake as he felt the cold steel of the pistol in his hands. He couldn't believe he was doing this. He hated himself for being weak enough to say he would shoot Joe. There was sweat on his hands as he raised the pistol. Joe didn't try to fly but looked directly at him. Their eyes met as Ben slid a finger onto the trigger.

'It looks like some of the crow's friends have come to watch!' Gary whispered in Luke's ear. 'A fiver says I could shoot the lot of them!'

Ben could see a dark shadow of crows sitting on the fence as he raised the pistol level with his shoulder.

'You can do this,' Ben murmured to himself as he tried to stop his hand from shaking. Joe was an easy target, but only Ben knew he had decided to miss. It would be his secret. Luke and Gary need never know. There was a crash as the shot rang out. The crows screamed as they took off from the fence. Joe flapped his wings but couldn't fly. He croaked with fear as he fell back to the ground. Something had hit him like a thunderbolt.

Ben cried out as he jumped forward to protect Joe. Then he told himself that it was his fault. He'd tried to miss but he couldn't even do that. One of Joe's wings was hurt. Feathers fluttered in the air like black snow. The crow closed its eyes in pain. A chorus of crows screeched overhead as they flapped into the sky. The crime had been witnessed.

'Finish it off!' Luke demanded as Ben stood over Joe. 'Smash a stone on its head. Knock its brains out!'

'You're not one of us if you don't!' Gary

yelled. 'And if you're not one of us you'll be strung up with that crow!'

Ben dropped the air pistol and picked up a large, flat stone. He turned sharply as he smashed it into Gary's ribs.

'I'm not one of you!' he screamed, knocking Gary to the ground. 'And I don't want to be! I don't like killing crows for fun. Just leave me and Joe alone!'

'It's a bit late for that!' Luke snarled as he seized Ben by the arm and twisted it behind his back. 'Get up, Gary! I need you to hold onto this little runt.'

Gary cursed as he struggled to his feet and gripped Ben by the throat.

'Just listen to it!' Luke said as he picked up the pistol and walked towards Joe.

'Anyone would think it was croaking for mercy. But how could it? It's just a stupid crow!'

Then Luke held the pistol to Joe's head and fired.

'You're scum!' Ben screamed from beneath Gary's grip. 'And that's something Ruth needs to know.'

There was no one in the street to see the two boys marching Ben off to Crow Hill. No one to notice the shadow of crows that circled the Meadow Estate before rising slowly into the sky.

Chapter Ten

The Keepers of Crow Law watched from the branches of the great oak tree as the three boys reached the top of Crow Hill. Two boys were dragging a smaller boy whose face was scratched and bleeding.

'Don't struggle, Crow Boy!' Luke ordered as he tightened his grip on Ben's collar. 'And there's no point screaming.

No one will hear you from here!'

Ben looked up at the still black shapes in the tree in front of him. Luke was right. Only the crows could see him. Only they could hear. The Meadow Estate was far away now, in the shadow of the hill.

'You ought to feel at home on Crow Hill!' Gary sniggered as he pushed Ben to the ground. 'Your feathered friends have roosted here for years.'

Ben felt his ankle twist beneath him as he fell. Then a cut above his eye started to bleed again and he could feel blood snaking down his face. The pain was bad, but it was nothing compared to the pain of shooting Joe and watching him suffer.

Ben thought about the injured bird as the punishment started. The boys laughed as they punched him. They tore his clothes as they pulled him onto their fists. They grinned as the beating went on. Then came the swearing as the boys spat in Ben's face. Ben didn't beg them to stop. Somehow he felt he deserved to suffer, just like Joe.

'We don't need city kids here!' Luke said savagely as he kicked Ben's head. 'Not soft kids who won't kill crows!'

Ben drifted in and out of consciousness as the boys spat on him and jeered. The world was spinning round him. The huge oak tree seemed to be rising and falling as hundreds of crows flew overhead.

Ben tried to move but couldn't. His arms and legs were numb. There was no strength left in his body. He just wanted to sleep and to forget. He'd let Joe down, and let himself down by shooting a bird just to fit in with the other kids. It was the biggest mistake of his life. The black shapes high in the tree screeched angrily as they gave their verdict.

Someone had broken Crow Law.

Ben heard a fluttering by his face and opened his eyes. A crow hopped onto his chest and for a moment he thought it was Joe.

'Good boy, Joe,' Ben whispered as the squawking of crows filled his ears. 'I'm so sorry I hurt you.'

Then Ben remembered the heap of black feathers stained with blood. Joe was dead. The world started to spin again as Ben raised his head. He screwed up his face as he tried to see. Then suddenly his eyes were wide open. Two huge crows stood on either side of his head.

'It's Crow Law!' Luke whispered as he and Gary backed away. 'Grandad says the blinding always comes first. It's the way of crows.'

'You said we'd just beat him up!' Gary

snapped back as Ben's screams tore through the air. 'Teach him a lesson, you said. But the kid can't move! We can't let this happen.'

Luke shrugged his shoulders and smiled. 'I can.'

Ben closed his eyes as he felt a rush of feathers on his face. He tried to scream again but found he could not breathe. Feathers were everywhere. On his skin and in his mouth.

'Help me, Luke!' Gary yelled as he flung himself at Ben and knocked the crows away with his fists. 'We've got to get him out of here. He needs a doctor!'

Luke sneered as Gary struggled to pull Ben to his feet. He watched them stagger into the distance until he was alone.

'Now don't they make a pretty couple,' he muttered to himself, with a snigger. 'Ben and Gary arm in arm! That'll give everyone a laugh at school!'

The Keepers of Crow Law watched the tall boy from the branches of the great oak tree. He was young and strong but their number was great. He would fight back, but the guilty could not go free.

There was a shudder in the sky as the black cloud descended. There was a whoosh of air and a beating of wings as the whole top of the great oak tree seemed to take flight.

Luke looked up as the shadow swooped over the sun. There were black beaks in the shadow and razor-sharp claws. Luke narrowed his eyes as the world suddenly turned dark as night.

He heard the cry that came from his throat when the crows spiralled downwards but knew that no one could help. He punched out with his fists but the blackness beat him to the ground with the power of hundreds of wings.

Luke's screams cut across the wind as the crows began their work. The blinding always came first. It was the way of crows. Then the real revenge could begin...

Look out for this exciting story
in the *Shades* series:

John Banks

The creature was on them before they had
a chance to run. They could make out a
shape in the dark. It walked on two legs,
and was as tall as a human being. A terrible
smell came from its body. Huge arms hung
down by its sides.

They all tried to turn and run towards
the hole in the fence but it was hard going
over the soft, sticky ground.

The creature snarled in anger. Its arm struck out at Luke, and he felt a blow on the side of the head. Luckily, it had hit him with the back of its hand, not its claws.

Suddenly Pete arrived with everyone from the camp. They carried torches and shone them on the creature from the other side of the fence.

At last they could see it. It was dark brown and scaly, with a face like a wolf. Its eyes were huge. White slime trailed from its jaws. A tail dragged along the ground. If there was such a place as hell, surely this creature must have come from it.

The creature seemed to hate the light. It covered its dazzled eyes with its arms.

Lisa could feel herself slipping in the mud. The creature was right behind her. She felt a terrible pain as one claw of its foot scratched her shoulder through her coat as she sprawled on the ground.

At that moment, Raven leapt for it. He had seen it attack his beloved Lisa. He sank his teeth into its scaly leg.

The dazzled creature couldn't see what was hurting it. It let out a dreadful shrieking howl. From behind the people by the fence came an answering howl. The other creature had come back.

There was instant panic. Everyone was desperate to escape. Running this way and that, they stumbled off through the woods, taking their torches with them.

Now the creature could see again. Frightened by the savage nip from Raven, it rushed towards the tunnel under the fence. Raven chased it, barking madly. Lisa managed to scramble up again.

'Raven! Come back!'

The creature coming down the path was

The creature snarled in anger. Its arm struck out at Luke, and he felt a blow on the side of the head. Luckily, it had hit him with the back of its hand, not its claws.

Suddenly Pete arrived with everyone from the camp. They carried torches and shone them on the creature from the other side of the fence.

At last they could see it. It was dark brown and scaly, with a face like a wolf. Its eyes were huge. White slime trailed from its jaws. A tail dragged along the ground. If there was such a place as hell, surely this creature must have come from it.

The creature seemed to hate the light. It covered its dazzled eyes with its arms.

Lisa could feel herself slipping in the mud. The creature was right behind her. She felt a terrible pain as one claw of its foot scratched her shoulder through her coat as she sprawled on the ground.

At that moment, Raven leapt for it. He had seen it attack his beloved Lisa. He sank his teeth into its scaly leg.

The dazzled creature couldn't see what was hurting it. It let out a dreadful shrieking howl. From behind the people by the fence came an answering howl. The other creature had come back.

There was instant panic. Everyone was desperate to escape. Running this way and that, they stumbled off through the woods, taking their torches with them.

Now the creature could see again. Frightened by the savage nip from Raven, it rushed towards the tunnel under the fence. Raven chased it, barking madly. Lisa managed to scramble up again.

'Raven! Come back!'

The creature coming down the path was

much braver than the one that had hurt Lisa. It forced its way through the hole cut in the fence.

Harold was still standing near the hole. The new creature decided to make him a target. Harold cried out in alarm. He could only just make out the creature's shape in the dark, but he knew that the wicked claws were coming towards his face.

Suddenly there was the roar of an engine. The generator! The floodlights flickered and came on. The whole scene was as bright as day. The creature screamed and put its paws over its eyes. With a huge leap, it reached the pit and slithered down inside.

Harold was dazzled too. He took a step back and slipped on the wet mud. He started to slide feet first down the hole. There was nothing to hold onto to stop him falling. Lisa was the nearest. She threw herself down on the ground and grabbed his hands just as they disappeared over the edge of the hole.

Harold was too heavy for her, but she wouldn't let go until she felt herself sliding down as well. When she did let go, it was too late. She was sliding head-first down the hole, with no idea how deep it was, or what was at the bottom.